Cinderella

Once upon a time there was a good-natured, pretty girl who was very much loved by her parents.

Unfortunately, her mother died of a sickness.

"Oh Mother, please don't go!" the poor daughter cried day after day. So her father decided to marry again to give her a new mother.

The step-mother brought two daughters with her. After the father left on a journey, the step-mother and the daughters became cruel to the girl.

They took away her nice clothes, gave her old rags to wear and made her work from morning till night.

A single piece of bread and a few peas were all she was given as a meal. They scattered the peas over the cinders and made the poor girl pick them up.

"There you go, pick them up and eat," said the cruel step-sisters and laughed at her. They called the poor girl Cinderella, which meant `ash girl'.

One day, what was worse, she received the sad news that her father had died during his journey. Now the step-mother drove her from her own room into a dim attic.

One day, invitations came from the palace for the family to attend a ball which the king was giving for his son, the prince.

The step-sisters became very excited and spent every day choosing ball gowns. They threw the invitation for Cinderella into the fire and said, "Cinderella, how could you go to the ball in your old rags?"

The sisters, in their best attire, went to the ball. Cinderella was left behind.

"I know I can't go to the ball in such old rags, but I wish I could..."

She began to cry because she was so sad at being all alone in the house. Her friends, the mouse and the cat, came to cheer her up.

Suddenly, she heard a voice say, "Stop crying, Cinderella."

Cinderella turned around and there she found a fairy.

"Now Cinderella, I am your Fairy Godmother and you shall go to the ball."

The fairy took her out to the pumpkin patch. When the fairy waved her magic wand over the finest pumpkin, it turned into a glittering golden coach. Four little mice became four handsome horses and two lizards found themselves changed into two fine footmen.

"Now, it's your turn, Cinderella," said the fairy and, with a wave of her magic wand, Cinderella was in a gorgeous dress fit for a princess.

"How beautiful!" Cinderella could not help dancing for joy and the fairy gave her a pair of glass slippers, the finest in the world.

"Remember," said the fairy, "leave the ball before the clock strikes twelve, or you will lose everything."

"I promise I will," replied Cinderella and got into the coach.

The golden coach went off to the palace where the ball was being held. Cinderella could not believe her good fortune.

The moment Cinderella entered the hall of the palace, everyone gasped at her extraordinary beauty.

"I wonder which country she belongs to?" everyone asked. There were many excited whispers and guesses. The prince came to her and extended his hand, saying, "Would you care to dance with me?"

While they were waltzing gracefully, the two sisters sighed and said, "The prince dances with nobody but the princess!"

They never imagined the princess was their step-sister.

The prince and Cinderella were dancing so happily they forgot all about the time. Then Cinderella heard the clock striking the hour of twelve.

"I must go now. Farewell, Your Highness!"

With these words, she fled from the ballroom.

The prince followed her, but he found only one of the glass slippers she had lost in her haste.

By the time the clock had struck twelve times, all the magic had disappeared.

Cinderella found herself in her rags again, but she was filled with joy.

"Thank you, Fairy Godmother! I had a wonderful time at the ball," she said to herself.

At the same time, in the palace, the prince was holding the little slipper and making up his mind.

"I will find your owner somehow," he vowed.

The next morning the prince proclaimed that he would find the girl whose foot fitted the slipper. The royal messengers took the slipper all over the kingdom and tried it on every girl, but in vain. They finally came to Cinderella's house. The two sisters tried to squeeze their feet into the slipper, but they could not make it fit. When the men asked Cinderella to try it on, the sisters laughed and said, "It will never fit her! She's just the maid!"

But Cinderella's foot went in smoothly.

"So, you are the princess we have been looking for!"
Before the man had spoken the last word, the fairy
appeared and waved her magic wand.

Cinderella's old rags turned into a wedding gown of
pure white.

"This gown will not disappear at twelve o'clock, my
dear," said the fairy. Cinderella was taken to the
palace and warmly welcomed by the prince.

Their wedding was held immediately
with celebrations attended by all the
citizens, and they lived happily ever
after.

First published by Joie, Inc.
Published by Peter Haddock Ltd,
Bridlington, England.
© Shogo Hirata
Printed and bound in Italy.